Happy reading!
Kelly Lenihan

Goober and Muffin

Story by Kelly Lenihan

Illustrations by Oona Risling-Sholl

ARTISAN BOOKWORKS

Artisan Bookworks
PO Box 1972
Sequim Washington 98382

Goober and Muffin/Kelly Lenihan. — 1st ed.
Published 1/2015
LCCN 2014954969
ISBN 978-0989869287

Printed in the United States of America

Goober and Muffin is dedicated to my two amazing boys, Christopher and Padraic, and all children who love stories.

Goober and Muffin were the best of friends. It did not matter that Goober was a puppy and Muffin was a kitten.

Goober and Muffin loved to run and play all day. Goober thought it was great fun to bat at Muffin's tail as she leaped out of reach, quickly turning around and going after Goober's tail.

Muffin liked to ride around on Goober's back as they people-watched or chased butterflies in their favorite park.

Their favorite game
to play was hide-and-
seek, although no
matter how cleverly
Muffin hid, Goober
always sniffed her out!

Goober and Muffin, Muffin and Goober.
Best friends forever.

As Goober and Muffin grew up, their friends started complaining that it was not okay for them to be pals.

"It is *not* socially acceptable for a cat and a dog to be friends" sniffed an uppity Siamese. "It just isn't done!"

Goober and Muffin were very sad. They really were best friends, but they did not want to hurt their other friends' feelings, so Goober and Muffin started spending less and less time together.

Goober tried hanging out with the other dogs, but they just weren't as fun as Muffin. No one could chase Goober or make him laugh like Muffin could.

Goober began spending more and more time wandering around alone.

Muffin tried to be a good sport. She did all the things cats were supposed to do, but mostly the other cats just sat around gossiping and preening themselves.

It was extremely boring and Muffin really missed her best friend Goober.

One day Muffin tagged along
with the other cats as they
crossed a small footbridge
leading to a tiny island in the
middle of the park.

Clouds rolled in and a storm came quickly, catching the cats off guard. They ran for shelter under some trees, huddling miserably in the downpour.

The rain thundered down and the river quickly swelled with water. All of a sudden the tiny bridge washed away, stranding the cats on the island.

Goober had seen the cats crossing the bridge earlier. When the storm washed the bridge away, he ran to the edge of the river, looking for Muffin.

As soon as Muffin saw Goober, she meowed loudly, calling for help. She was very frightened when she saw Goober running away.

Goober did not run away though, he went to get help. Goober ran swiftly to find the other dogs, barking mightily.

Realizing that there was trouble, the dogs followed Goober back to the river and saw the trapped cats huddled together, wet and shivering.

Goober carefully crossed the swirling water and lay down next to Muffin so that she could climb onto his back, just as she did when they were playing.

Watching Goober and Muffin, the rest of the cats quickly latched onto the backs of the other dogs.

Goober slowly re-crossed the water, returning to safety on the other side of the river, with the other dogs and cats right behind him.

Goober and Muffin were so happy to see each other. They hugged and nuzzled and rolled around together, not caring that the ground was wet and muddy.

Realizing that their friendship meant more to Goober and Muffin than the fact that they looked different from each other, they decided right then and there that being best friends was more important than anything their misguided friends thought.

Goober and Muffin, Muffin and Goober. Best friends forever.

Thank you for add ing *Goober and Muffin* to your library.

If your child enjoyed this story, please consider posting a thoughful review on Amazon.com on your child's behalf.

Your kindness will make a difference for other readers considering this book.

In gratitude,
Kelly

Hi Kids,

Send me a letter or draw me a picture,
I'd love to hear from you!

Kelly Lenihan
PO Box 1972
Sequim WA 98383

Ask a grown-up to help you download
coloring pages from *Goober and Muffin*
as well as other fun activity sheets.

www.kellylenihanbooks.com/for-kids/

Happy coloring!

ABOUT THE AUTHOR

Kelly Lenihan

As a child, Kelly was forever dreaming up fantastical stories, inventing make-believe worlds replete with colorful characters engaging in wondrous adventures. By the end of her teens, she'd written countless short stories. Never losing her penchant for writing; she's been published in various magazines and enjoyed her own newspaper column for several years. To this day, she is an avid blogger and has several full-length books in the works as well as more picture books. As a parent, Kelly shared her love of the magical world of books by reading aloud to her two boys, sometimes making up stories on the fly. *Goober and Muffin* is one of those stories and it remains a beloved family favorite. She hopes you love it too.

Visit www.kellylenihanbooks.com for more books by Kelly, including *The Skipping Stone*, and to find out what she's working on now!

ABOUT THE ILLUSTRATOR

Oona Risling-Sholl

Oona is an autodidactic artist hailing from foggy northern California. Her portfolio includes painting, drawing, and printmaking, as well as graphic art and poster design. She has also designed theater sets and backdrops for troupes and events throughout Northern California. This is Oona's second time illustrating a children's book.

CPSIA information can be obtained at www.ICGtesting.com
Printed in the USA
BVOW11*1903151214

379507BV00010B/15/P